TOUCHSTONE

Other Books by
RICHARD BRAUTIGAN

Novels

Trout Fishing in America
A Confederate General from Big Sur
In Watermelon Sugar
The Abortion: An Historical Romance 1966
The Hawkline Monster: A Gothic Western

Poetry

The Galilee Hitch-Hiker *
Lay the Marble Tea *
The Octopus Frontier *
All Watched Over by Machines of Loving Grace *
Please Plant This Book
The Pill Versus the Springhill Mine Disaster
Rommel Drives on Deep into Egypt

Short Stories

Revenge of the Lawn

* out of print

Willard and His Bowling Trophies

A Perverse Mystery

Richard Brautigan

A Touchstone Book Published by
Simon and Schuster

Copyright © 1975 by Richard Brautigan
All rights reserved
including the right of reproduction
in whole or in part in any form
A Touchstone Book
Published by Simon and Schuster
A Division of Gulf & Western Corporation
Simon & Schuster Building
Rockefeller Center
1230 Avenue of the Americas
New York, New York 10020

Designed by Elizabeth Woll
Manufactured in the United States of America

1   2   3   4   5   6   7   8   9   10

Library of Congress Cataloging in Publication Data

Brautigan, Richard.
    Willard and his bowling trophies.

    I. Title.
PZ4.B826Wi [PS3503.R2736]   813'.5'4   75-5991
ISBN 0-671-22065-9
ISBN 0-671-22745-9 pbk.

"The dice of Love are madnesses and melees."

—Anacreon
The *Greek Anthology*

"This land is cursed with violence."

—Senator Frank Church
Democrat, Idaho

Willard and His
Bowling Trophies

The Greek Anthology

Constance turned herself awkwardly on the bed to watch him leave the room.

"I've been thinking about this all day long," Bob said. "I want you—" Then he was gone with his voice trailing away, "to hear it," down the hall to another room.

She lay there awkwardly waiting for him to return. She thought that he was only going to be gone for a moment but he was gone for almost ten minutes.

The air in the bedroom was warm and still. It was an unusually warm September evening in San Francisco but the window was closed and the shades were down.

They had to be.

He can't find the book, she thought.

He was always losing things. For many long months

now he'd had a lot of trouble doing anything right. It made her sad because she loved him.

She sighed, which became a slight muffled sound because of the handkerchief that was loosely stuffed in her mouth. She could have easily pushed the hand- kerchief out of her mouth with her tongue if she had wanted to.

Bob couldn't do anything right now.

He couldn't even gag her well.

But of course he had tied her hands too tight and her feet too loose and she sighed again, making a muffled sound as she waited for him to find the book that he'd lost which was usual for everything he did now.

He hadn't always been this way and she felt guilty about it because she thought that it was partly her fault for giving him the warts and after he got the warts, all of this stuff started happening.

The light hanging down from the ceiling should have been a hundred-watt bulb, but instead it was a two-hun- dred-watt bulb. It was his doing. She didn't like that much light. He did.

Finally he came back into the room with the book and she pushed the gag out of her mouth and said, "My hands are too tight."

"Oh," he said, looking down at her from the book in his hand which was turned to a particular page that he was just about to read aloud.

He put the book down on the bed, still opened to the page that he wanted to read from. He sat down beside her and she rolled awkwardly over onto her stomach, so that

12

he could get at the knot in the rope. She didn't have any clothes on and she had a nice body.

He retied her hands so that they weren't as tight, but they were still tight enough so that she couldn't get them loose.

"Retie my feet," she said. "They're too loose."

If he's going to be an amateur sadist, she thought, *I might as well see if I can get him to do it right.*

She was very disappointed in him. She was a perfectionist in everything that she did and was very annoyed with his newly found incompetence.

For months now, ever since he had gone on his amateur sadist trip, she had been thinking: *Anybody can tie up somebody and gag them, why can't he?*

Why can't he do anything right and he overwaters the plants and things drop out of his hands and he's always falling over things and breaking things and he forgets what he's talking about half the time in the middle of what he's saying but I guess it really doesn't make that much difference because he doesn't talk about anything interesting, anyway, and it's been going on for months, ever since she gave him the warts, but hadn't she suffered with them, too, going to the doctor all those times and having the warts burned off in her vagina with an electric needle and then coming home on the bus, holding back the tears in a lonely moving place filled with silent strangers? . . . oh, God . . . oh, well . . . we could be dead. Maybe this is better than being dead, I guess. I don't know.

After he finished tying her feet again, he started to pick up the book that he had been about to read from.

Then he noticed that the gag was out of her mouth. He put the book back down and leaned over toward her. She knew what he wanted and what he was going to do.

She opened her mouth as wide as she could.

He suddenly got nervous. Sometimes when he gagged her he pushed part of the gag against her lower lip with his thumb and he would hurt her mouth as it was going in and she would really get mad at him and curse him, "BASTARD!" Then the gag would be in her mouth and her curses would be muffled, inarticulate, but he knew what she was saying and it always made him feel bad and sometimes he would blush and his ears would tingle with embarrassment.

She would glower up at him from beautiful green eyes. He would turn away from them and wait for her to calm down.

He didn't like being an incompetent but there was nothing that he could do about it. It had been going on for months and it didn't make him feel very good either.

He could tell by how wide she had just opened her mouth that he had better control his nervousness and not hurt her when he put the gag back in her mouth.

Her mouth was delicate, her tongue sculptured and pink. The gag was already very wet from her spit. He put it carefully back into her mouth, making sure that he did not hurt her with his thumb. He took his index finger and worked the gag back into all the crevices of her mouth.

She lay there on her stomach with her hands tied behind her back, resting just above her ass. Her head was arched back now, so she would be in a better position for him to gag her.

14

They had done this many times.

The room was illuminated by a light that was too bright.

She had long blonde hair.

There was just a small piece of the gag sticking out between her teeth. He very carefully tucked that piece into her mouth. Then he gave the gag a good push with his finger straight back into her mouth, so as to make her tongue totally immobile, useless to push the gag out with.

He was very nervous and he tried to control it because he didn't want to hurt her but he also wanted the gag to be firmly in her mouth.

She moaned behind the gag when he started pushing it back into place with his finger. She moved her head suddenly side to side as if to escape the finger that was pushing the gag against her tongue.

He continued pushing for a few more seconds and then he knew it was in place and she would not be able to work it out with her tongue.

About once in every ten times he would gag her effectively. He just didn't have it together any more. He knew that his failures annoyed her, but what else could he do?

His whole life was a sloppy and painful mess.

He had used adhesive tape for a while. The tape always gagged her effectively but she didn't like the way it hurt when he pulled it off. Even if he pulled it off very gently, it still hurt like hell, so the tape had to go.

"No," she had said about the tape and he knew that it was no. She had never said no before, so he stopped using the tape.

He took his finger out of her mouth and stroked the side of her face. She relaxed her head. He stroked her hair. She stared silently up at him. She really had very beautiful eyes. Everybody always mentioned that to her. She awkwardly crawled and inched her body over to him. It was difficult but she got her head up onto his lap and she was staring up at him. Her hair poured over his lap like blonde water.

She really loved him.

That's what made it all so bad.

"Can you breathe all right?" he said.

She nodded her head gently that she could breathe all right.

"Does the gag hurt?"

She shook her head gently that the gag did not hurt.

"Do you want to hear what I read today?"

She nodded her head gently that she wanted to hear what he had read today.

He picked up the book.

It was a very old book.

He read to her: " 'O Poverty, thou grievous and resistless ill, who with thy sister Helplessness overwhelmest a great people . . .' "

She stared up at him.

"That's Alcaeus from the *Greek Anthology*," he said. "That was written over two thousand years ago."

. . . *oh, God,* she thought and tried very hard not to cry because she knew if she started crying that would make him feel even worse and he had been feeling pretty bad for a long time.

The *Story of* O

Constance and Bob's fourth-rate theater of sadism and despair started off rather simply. She was the first one to get the warts. They were venereal warts inside of her vagina.

She'd had a drunken one-night-stand love affair with a middle-aged lawyer who had read her book. She was a twenty-three-year-old-just-failed novelist and he had told her that he liked her book and she was feeling very badly because the book, though it was a critical success, was not selling, and she had been forced to go back to work.

So she went to bed with the lawyer and got warts in her vagina.

They looked like a hideous clump of nightmare mushrooms. They had to be burned off with an electric needle:

one painful treatment following on the claws of another painful treatment.

When she found out that she had the warts, she talked to Bob about ending their marriage. She felt so embarrassed. She thought that there was no reason to continue her life.

"Please . . ." she said. "I can't go on living with you. I've done such a terrible thing."

"No way," Bob told her and was so good to her, knowing all about the affair, and he took care of everything in a super-effective way which was how he handled things . . . then.

They could not have a normal sex life for two months because that's how long it took for the warts to be burned out of her vagina and sometimes when she came home from seeing the doctor and his electric needle, she would just sit down and start crying.

Bob comforted her and took care of her and made her feel better, caressing her hair, holding her, talking gently to her, "You're my woman. I love you. It will be all over soon," until she stopped crying.

Because they were denied access to a traditional sex life, venereal warts are caused by a communicable virus that's transmitted through intercourse, they had to do other things, which they did.

They really liked having intercourse together. Bob loved the way his penis fit inside of Constance's vagina, and she did, too. They used to make jokes about erotic plumbing. They were both kind of traditional sex fiends.

One day somebody loaned Bob a copy of the Story of O, which he read. It is a gothic sadomasochist novel that sort of turned him on because he thought that it was so strange. He would get a partial erection when he read it.

After he finished the book, he gave it to Constance to read because she was curious about it.

"What's it about?" she asked.

She read it and got sort of turned on, too.

"It's kind of sexy," she said.

A week after they had both finished reading it, they were drunkish one evening and sexually playing around in their special ways because they were denied the regular sex act.

Usually, she would jack him off or orally copulate him and he would very carefully, like cutting a diamond, clitorally masturbate her until she came. He could have gotten a job at Tiffany's.

They were lying there in bed, sort of drunk, when he said, "Why don't we play the *Story of O*?"

"OK," Constance said, smiling. "Which part do I play?"

The *Story of O* Game

They had a lot of fun playing the *Story of O* game for the
first time. Constance found some scarfs for him to tie her
up with and she found a large silk handkerchief for him to
gag her with. Bob tied a knot in the center of the handkerchief as he had seen on television and in the movies
and put the knot between her teeth and tied the ends of
the handkerchief tightly at the back of her head, so that
her mouth was forced open by the knot.

Her hands were tied behind her back.

She was breathing very heavily. She had never been
tied and gagged before. He caressed her breasts and her
thighs. She liked the feeling of helplessness and pleasure.

Then he whipped her very gently with his belt and
she moaned pleasurably from behind the gag. While all

this was happening, he still had his clothes on. She lay naked on the bed.

After a while he took his clothes off and joined her on the bed. She rubbed up against him, moaning all the time through the gag. She was very excited. He put his finger on her clitoris diamondly, so as to avoid touching the burned-off wart areas and hurting her.

He was not interested in hurting her.

Bob rolled Constance over, so that her back was to him, and he guided her bound hands to his penis and he had his left hand touching her clitoris and his right hand caressing her right breast, which was quite beautiful, not too small and not too large: with a small pink-rose nipple.

Constance awkwardly and beautifully jacked him off while he masturbated her carefully and beautifully and they almost came together.

Their bodies raged like an apocalypse of fire, pleasure, and small-time perversion.

Warts

When the warts were discovered inside of Constance's vagina, Bob checked himself out for them, but there weren't any warts on his penis.

Venereal warts are spread by a virus through sexual intercourse, but only a small percentage of the people who come in contact with the virus actually get them, so some people will carry the virus and not get the warts and some people will come in contact with the virus without getting them.

Bob was very relieved that he did not have them. Weeks passed and no warts appeared on his penis, so they assumed that he would not get them, but then one night when she was almost clear of them, he was peeing and discovered that he had some warts inside of his penis.

It had never dawned on him to look inside of his penis, down into the urethra. The warts were like an evil little island of pink mucous roses. He couldn't believe it. He stood there staring at the warts in his penis. He thought that he was going to throw up.

Long after he had finished peeing, he was still standing there above the toilet bowl, staring at his penis.

Then he put it back into his pants as if he were folding a dead octopus tentacle into his shorts and flushed the toilet.

The urine swirled like an evil punctuation mark and disappeared. The sun was going down, too. He waited for Constance to come home from visiting a friend. The apartment was very quiet. He didn't turn the lights on. Normally, he hated the dark. He stared out the window at the early evening traffic that sounded like rain. He shivered as if he were cold. The cars passing down below made him think of a very lonely rainy afternoon in his childhood.

He went back there again.

When she opened the door with her key and came in, the apartment was dark, so she turned a light on. She didn't think he was there. He was sitting in the room a few feet away from her, staring out the window with eyes that looked as if they had transparent lead in them.

"What's wrong?" she said.

"I've got warts in my cock," he said.

She sat down very carefully on the floor beside him as if she were sitting on a decayed spider web.

"Deeply Do I Mourn, for My Friends Are Nothing Worth"

"These are just fragments," Bob said, almost a year later to Constance lying bound and gagged on a bed without any clothes on, her head resting in his lap.

"Lines," he said. "Parts of lines . . ." He paused and then forgot for a moment what he was talking about.

Constance waited for him to remember what he was talking about. He was turning the pages of the book but he didn't know why. They turned like leaves in an absent-minded wind.

Then he remembered what he was doing and started over again, repeating the very same words that he had just used. "These are just fragments. Lines," he said. "Parts of lines and sometimes only single words that remain from the original poems written by the Greeks thousands of years ago."

" 'More beautiful,' " Bob said. "That's all that's left of a poem."

" 'Having fled,' " Bob said. "That's all that's left of another one."

" 'He cheats you,' " Bob said. " 'Breaking.' 'You have made me forget all my sorrows.' There are three more."

"Here are two really beautiful ones," Bob said. 'Deeply do I mourn, for my friends are nothing worth.' 'Takes bites of the cucumbers.' "

"What do you think? Do you like them?" Bob said. He had forgotten that she could not answer him. She nodded her head yes that she liked them.

"Would you like to hear some more?" Bob said.

He had forgotten that there was a gag in her mouth.

She slowly nodded yes.

"Here are four more fragments," Bob said. "They are all that remain of a man's voice from thousands of years ago: 'Storms.' 'Of these.' 'I was.' 'He understood.' Incredible, huh?"

She very slowly nodded yes.

"One more?" Bob asked.

She slowly nodded yes.

" 'And nothing will come of anything,' " Bob said.

Willard and His
Bowling Trophies

What about Willard and his bowling trophies? How do they figure into this tale of perversion? Easy. They were in an apartment downstairs.

Willard was a papier-mâché bird about three feet tall with long black legs and a partially black body covered with a strange red, white and blue design like nothing you've ever seen before, and Willard had an exotic beak like a stork. His bowling trophies were of course stolen.

They were stolen from three brothers, the Logan brothers, who had formed a very good, actually a championship bowling team that they played on for years. Bowling was their life's blood and then somebody stole all their trophies.

The Logan brothers had been looking for them ever

since, travelling around the country like three evil brothers in a Western.

They were lean, sharp-eyed and seedy-looking from letting their clothes fall into disrepair and from not shaving regularly and they had turned into vicious criminals to finance their search for the stolen trophies.

They had started out in life as wholesome all-American boys, an inspiration to young and old alike, showing how you could make something out of your life and be looked up to. Unfortunately, the torment of three lost years looking for their bowling trophies had changed them. They were a far cry from the Logan brothers of old: those handsome heroic bowlers and the pride of their hometown.

Willard of course always stayed the same: a papier-mâché bird surrounded by his bowling trophies.

"And Nothing
Will Come
of Anything"

The room was too bright. It was not a large room, and the light bulb hanging down from the ceiling was too big for the room. Cars passed down below in the street. The street had a lot of traffic early in the evening.

He stared down at her.

Bob's face was very gentle and distant and dreaming backwards. He was thinking about people who lived in another time and were dead now and he grieved for them and himself and the entire human condition: the past and future of it all.

Constance, staring up at him, was deeply moved by the expression on his face.

Suddenly she wanted to tell him that she loved him, even though he had come to this, but she couldn't. Only about one out of every ten times was he able to effectively gag her and this had to be that time.

What luck, she thought.

So she caressed his leg with her cheek which was all that she could do to tell him that she loved him. She wanted to tell him that they would get through this and put it all back together and make it beautiful again, but she couldn't because her tongue was pressed hard against the back of her mouth by a handkerchief soaking wet with her own spit.

She closed her eyes.

" 'And nothing will come of anything,' " Bob softly repeated again but this time only to himself.

The Logan Brothers
in Pursuit

One of the Logan brothers sat in a chair drinking a can of
beer. Another one lay on the bed in the cheap hotel room
reading a comic book. From time to time he laughed out
loud. The aging wallpaper looked like the skin of a snake.
His laughter rattled off the walls.

The third brother paced back and forth in the room,
which was a slight feat in itself because the room was so
small. He was displeased by his brother laughing at the
comic book. He thought that his brother should not aban-
don himself to such easy pastimes.

"Where are those God-damn bowling trophies?" he
yelled.

The Logan brother on the bed dropped his comic
book in surprise and the one drinking beer stopped the

can in mid-flight to his mouth and turned it into the statue of a beer can.

They stared at their brother who was still pacing impossibly in the tiny room.

"Where are those God-damn bowling trophies?" he repeated.

They were waiting for a telephone call that would tell them where the bowling trophies were. The telephone call was costing them $3,000, money that had been earned from panhandling, misdemeanor thievery, then filling station hold-ups and finally murder.

It had been a long three years they had spent in search of the trophies. The Logan brothers' all-American innocence had been one of its casualties.

"Where are those God-damn bowling trophies?"

Saint Willard

Meanwhile—less than a mile away from the tiny dingy hotel room where the Logan brothers waited for a telephone call that would provide them with the location of the bowling trophies—Willard, a huge papier-mâché bird, stood leaning up against the trophies. There were about fifty or so of them sitting on the floor: large elaborate ones like miniature bowling altars and small ones like ikons.

Willard and the bowling trophies were in the front room of a big apartment. It was night and dark in the front room but even so there was a faint religious glow coming from the bowling trophies.

Saint Willard of the Stolen Bowling Trophies!

The people who lived in the apartment were off

seeing a Greta Garbo rerun at a local art theater. Their names were John and Patricia. He was a young filmmaker and she was a school teacher. They were very good friends with their upstairs neighbors Constance and Bob.

Bob would come down by himself three or four times a week. He liked to sit in the front room on the floor with Willard and his bowling trophies and drink coffee and talk with John about Willard. Pat would usually be off teaching. She taught Spanish at a junior high school.

Bob would ask questions about Willard and his metal friends. Often it would be the same question because Bob would forget that he'd asked it before.

"Where did you get these bowling trophies?" Bob asked for the hundredth time or was it the thousandth time? It was his favorite question to ask over and over again.

"I found them in an abandoned car in Marin County," John would patiently answer for the hundredth or was it the thousandth time? John had known Bob for three years now and Bob had not been like this when John first knew him. Bob had been very skillful with all the aspects of his life and had a mind so sharp that it could have picnicked on a razor blade.

It bothered John to see Bob this way. He hoped that it would pass and Bob would be like he used to be.

John sometimes wondered what had happened to cause Bob to act this way: always asking the same questions over and over again, "Where did you get these bowling trophies?" etc., moving awkwardly about and being absent-minded and sometimes he tipped his coffee over

33

and John would clean it up and Bob would barely be conscious that he had done it.

Bob had once been a hero to John because he had been so good at doing and saying things. Those days were gone and John longed for them to return.

The bowling trophies continued glowing faintly in the room where Willard was a shadow among them like an unspoken prayer.

John and Pat would be back later on, talking about Greta Garbo, and turn the front room light on and there would be faithful Willard and his bowling trophies.

"Celery"

Bob took his belt off and slowly began to whip Constance with it: leaving slight red marks across her buttocks and the backs of her legs. She moaned abstractly from behind her gag, which was firmly in her mouth and she could not spit it out.

Sometimes it still turned her on when he whipped her. It had really turned her on the first few times he had done it to her when they had played the *Story of O* game before he had gotten the warts in his penis and they wouldn't go away.

He never broke the flesh when he whipped her or left any bruises on her body. He was very careful about that. He was not interested in hurting her.

Whipping her did not turn him on nearly as much as

tying her up and gagging her, but he went on doing it as part of the ritual that led up to their very pathetic sex act because he liked to hear her moan from behind the gag.

The thing that she really didn't like about it was being gagged but that was the part of it that turned him on the most and the part of it that he was the worst at doing because he got so excited and nervous when he did it. She could never figure out why he concentrated so much on the gagging and he never told her because he didn't know himself.

Sometimes he tried to figure out why he liked gagging her but he couldn't find a rational reason. He just liked it and did it.

Many times after he had finished tying her up, which was always what he did first, she would say, "Please don't gag me. It's all right to tie me up and to whip me but please don't gag me. Please. I don't like it," but he would do it anyway and most of the time he bungled it and sometimes he hurt her and it was very seldom that she liked being gagged and those few, very rare times were only because she remembered liking it in the beginning.

Then he put the belt down beside her on the bed. That part was over.

Her eyes were beautiful above the gag, he thought, so sensitive and intelligent staring at him.

He untied her feet.

" 'Let us put little garlands of celery upon our brows and hold high festival to Dionysus,' " Bob said to her, quoting the *Greek Anthology* from memory.

"Pretty, huh?" he said.

She closed her eyes.

Rubber

Bob still had his clothes on but he could feel the erection in his pants. It bulged and pressed hard against his leg. Now the time was nearing that he really dreaded.

The only way he could enter her vagina with his penis so that she wouldn't get the warts again was to use a rubber which he hated and she hated.

He walked over to a dresser and hidden under his socks was a package of rubbers. He fumbled a rubber out of the package. He felt dirty touching it.

Constance was watching him from the bed.

She knew how much he hated using them.

Bob came back to the bed. He took his clothes off. He had a tall, healthy body. Looking at his body, there was no way of knowing that he had warts in his penis.

He took the foil-packed rubber and broke the foil and took the horrible thing out and was slightly nauseated by the smell of the thing. He really hated that rubber smell. He shuddered when he fit the rubber over his penis and did not look at Constance while he was doing it.

Putting the rubber on always embarrassed him and she looked away, too, not wanting to see this embarass-ment.

The rubber was on and he felt like a damn fool.

The Logan Brothers
Waiting

The comic-book-reading Logan brother put the comic book down on the bed beside him. He stared at the cover. The hero on it looked somber as a stale cookie.

The beer-drinking Logan brother finished one beer and started on another one. He liked feeling the cold of the can in his hand. It was one of the few pleasures he had left after three years of looking for the stolen bowling trophies.

The pacing Logan brother was walking up and down the tiny room. He had a revolver in his hand. He kept opening and closing the loaded cylinder, staring at the bullets. He was anxious to use the gun. He wanted to kill the people who had taken his beloved bowling trophies.

They would pay dearly . . .

With their lives!

Soon the telephone would ring. It sat darkly on a table like graves waiting to be dug.

The comic-book-reading Logan brother reopened the comic book to an ad for selling salve in your spare time and on your way home from school. He read the ad very carefully. He wondered how it would be to sell salve.

Kissing

She hated the feeling of the rubber going into her vagina. She really had to be moist or it would hurt. He had such a beautiful penis. It had been so long since she had felt it inside of her. All she had felt for almost a year now was the rubber instead of him. It was a nightmare and he couldn't do anything right any more.

Oh, God!

She rubbed her gagged mouth against his mouth in a tender kissing gesture.

"Painting a Lion from the Claw"

He couldn't feel her and it always made him sad but that was nothing new because just about everything made him sad now. The rubber took away all the intimacy and eternity of her vagina. He hungered like a lost star for the evening sky of her inner touch.

He was gently inside of her but he couldn't feel her. She was lost from him, so he thought about the *Greek Anthology* and remembered words from ancient times that said, "Painting a lion from the claw."

What did it mean to him thinking about that as he rested upon her, trying to make love? What good would it do him to think of things like that?

He didn't know.

Willard,
the Bowling Trophies
and Greta Garbo

They were talking as they came up the stairs.

"Greta Garbo looked so beautiful," John said.

"She was really a great actress," Pat said.

"Too bad Connie and Bob couldn't come with us," John said.

John's key opened the front door lock and Pat pushed the door open. Across the room was the darkened outline of Willard like a dwarf tree and the religiously glowing bowling trophies.

The *click* of the light switch exploded Willard and the trophies into their full presence and the glory in that presence.

Willard looked curious. Sometimes the expression on Willard's face would change. He was artfully constructed.

"Hi, Willard," Pat said. "You would have loved Greta Garbo. Hey, we should have taken Willard to see Greta Garbo."

"Next time," John said. "We'll put Willard in a child's dress and get him in free. I can carry him in my arms. Nobody will notice."

"What about his beak?" Pat said.

"We'll think of something," John said.

The Birth
of Willard

Willard was made by an artist who lived in some isolated mountains in a part of California that was hard to find.

The artist was in his late thirties and had had a very fucked-up life with many bad love affairs and much torment but he had somehow kept it together and was now supporting himself from his sculpture and he had a woman who took care of his basic physical and spiritual wants without fooling with his head too much.

Willard came to him in a dream, a dream that was composed of miniature silver and gold temples built but never used and waiting for a religion.

Willard just walked right into the dream as if he had lived there forever with his long black legs and strangely-patterned body and of course his dynamic beak and his face that could almost change expressions.

Willard walked over and took a good look at the miniature silver and gold temples. Willard liked them. They would be his family and his home.

The next morning the artist took some papier-mâché and rags and paint and stuff and re-created Willard from his dream until Willard was standing there, separated and made real, ready to occupy his own life.

The History of
the Logan Brothers

The Logan brothers had come from a simple, very large family. Besides the three brothers and their mother and father, there were also three sisters. The sisters did not bowl. They had another specialty which will be gone into later.

Their father worked in a filling station as a mechanic. He was very good with cars. Transmissions were his specialty. People said that he had a Midas touch when it came to working with transmissions.

He had such a way with transmissions that he once fixed a transmission so well that when the man who owned the car, the chief of police, got into it and turned the engine on and shifted gears, he started crying because the transmission was in such great shape. The chief was not a man known for easy tears.

Mother Logan was a pleasant woman who minded her own business and did a lot of baking. She just loved to have her oven on. The house was always filled with cakes and pies and cookies.

The Logan brothers had a typical uneventful American childhood. They were no rougher or gentler than other boys. They had their share of illnesses and broken arms and getting into minor trouble or pleasing their parents with one thing or another.

Once they all got together and built their mother a birdhouse to put outside the window she looked out from while she was mixing her doughs, crusts, batters and frostings. The birdhouse pleased her a great deal.

Unfortunately, birds did not like the house and not a single bird ever used it, but still it was something to look at and she would look at it while she baked away.

Birds are not necessary for baking.

The only outstanding characteristic of the Logan brothers was their interest in bowling. The brothers just loved to bowl and they were good at it, too. There was a bowling alley a few blocks away from their house and it was like a second home to them.

Those bowling alleys were as familiar to them as their mother's baking. They all got shivers up and down their spines every time they touched a bowling ball, and the sound of crashing pins was music to their ears.

They formed a junior high school bowling team that won the state championship with a team average of 152, which of course led them to winning the first of their many bowling trophies. They thought that the most beautiful thing they had ever seen was that trophy.

You could say with a great deal of conviction that those boys had very little else except bowling on their minds.

At Home with the Bowling Trophies

By the time the Logan brothers were in their middle twenties, they had accumulated over fifty bowling trophies. They continued living in their parents' house and found various jobs in town and never went out with girls and devoted themselves like monks to bowling and like bankers to the gathering of trophies.

They used to sit around the house at night when they weren't out bowling and drink beer and stare affectionately at their bowling trophies.

The trophies were housed in a magnificent oak cabinet that was polished to such a shine that it was like a form of wooden gold. The glass doors to the cabinet were breathtaking. It is very rare for the doors to a cabinet to take your breath away.

The house was usually filled with the scent of something being baked in the kitchen and their father was always watching television after another day of fixing transmissions.

The Logan brothers had a good life because they were doing exactly what they wanted to do and they had their bowling trophies to show how good they were at their life.

Coming

It was pleasure, frustration and hatred when he came inside of her. There was a mud-like oozing explosion of release. Then the feeling of sperm confined against the end of his penis, held prisoner in the rubber. Sometimes he almost got sick at his stomach or felt like crying.

She had gotten so that she could come sometimes when he came. It was hard but sometimes she could do it. It always made her feel weird now when she came to his coming which was in the form of rubber. She felt as if she were making love to somebody who lived in another country.

Before the venereal warts visited their lives, sex had been to them like having a beautiful picnic in a field of comets. But now he spread-eagled her on the bed, tying her arms and legs to the four posts of the bed or he tied her hands behind her back. She didn't like to have her hands tied that way because it was very uncomfortable.

She didn't mind being spread-eagled if he didn't stretch her arms and legs out too tight, but sometimes he did. She "preferred" to have her hands tied directly above her head, but that didn't turn him on very often, so . . . actually, what she wanted was a long vacation from bondage and minor-league sadism. There was very little thrill to it any more and she wished that he didn't have the warts in his penis and he hadn't changed sexually and they could go back to fucking like they used to. She was not a sexual prude but she did not like their whole sex life devoted to sadism.

If only her novel had been a commercial success as well as a critical success and she hadn't felt so depressed and insecure that she had one-night-standed with the lawyer, even though she loved Bob very much, and brought the venereal warts home with her. Also, because her novel had failed, she had to go back to modelling, which she hated. She felt that it degraded her but Bob couldn't work any more because he was too abstract and she had to support him.

So now . . .

"Constance Marlow's novel After Class *shows great promise and it is a privilege to welcome her to American letters."*

—The New York Times Book Review

she "preferred" to have her hands tied

"Miss Marlow's book is a delight to read in a very sad way."

—Saturday Review

directly above her head

"Hurrah for Constance Marlow!"

—Chicago Tribune

but that didn't turn him on . . . so

"A brilliant young stylist goes to the head of her literary generation."

—Los Angeles Times

so . . .

Ritual

It always happened this way: After he came his penis would slowly soften inside of her and their bodies would be very quiet together like two haunted houses staring across a weedy vacant lot at each other. Then always with a slight feeling of abstract disgust, he would pull out of her, get up and take the rubber off, carefully not looking at it, with his back to her and leave the room, and he would walk dream-like down the hall to the toilet. He hated the way the wet warm rubber occupied his hand like a dirty joke from outer space.

Carefully looking away, he would drop the rubber into the toilet bowl and flush it, feeling by now terrible as if he had been part of something very obscene.

He would wash his penis very, very carefully, still not

looking at it, and then dry it with a special towel that he wouldn't allow Constance to use because he was afraid she might get the warts again and he couldn't stand that.

No, that would be too much.

It would be the end of him.

Then he would walk slowly, dream-like, back to where Constance lay, still bound and gagged, waiting for him to untie her, so they could go on with the rest of their life together.

Events Leading Up
to the

One evening the entire Logan family, except for the daughters who were elsewhere again, went to a drive-in movie. Their mother brought along a giant sack of cookies. Going to a movie was a very rare thing for them to do. They thought the picture they were going to see was about bowling, but it turned out to be about playing pool and starred Paul Newman.

The Logan brothers were very disappointed and could not figure out how they had made the mistake of thinking that the picture was about bowling when it was actually about playing pool.

They tried to blame it on one another.

"It's your fault," one of the Logan brothers accused another Logan brother.

"You're full of shit!" was the reply.

"Don't talk that way in front of your mother," was their father's immediate response to that remark. He had been listening to a transmission in one of the cars in the movie before his son started talking dirty.

"I'm sorry, Mom," was the apology.

"You're forgiven, son," was the acceptance.

"How could we have been so stupid to think that the movie was about bowling," one of the other brothers said, voicing extreme disappointment.

"Let's forget it. It's done," the Logan father said. "Have another cookie."

He was a Libra.

Theft of the Bowling Trophies

The disappointment of not seeing a bowling picture at the drive-in made the trip back home a very quiet one for the Logan brothers. They felt betrayed, especially because they knew that Paul Newman could make a hell-of-a-bowling movie if he wanted to.

When they walked into the house the bowling trophies were gone. It was that simple. The cabinet was cleaned out. It was completely void of bowling trophies. The cabinet looked like the toothless gums of an old man.

The Logan family stood in a half-circle around the cabinet not believing their eyes. They were silent miniature Mount Rushmores.

"SOMEBODY STOLE OUR BOWLING TROPHIES!!!"

finally broke the silence like a locomotive leaping its tracks and crashing into an ice-covered lake to sink instantly out of sight, leaving a giant steaming hole in its wake.

Bringing Her Back
to This World

Bob took the gag out of Constance's mouth. He took it out very carefully, so as not to hurt her. She thought this was considerate.

Her green eyes staring up at him.

The gag was so wet from her spit that it was almost like some kind of phantasmagorical cement. He worked it gently out of all the crevices of her mouth. Her tongue had been made completely useless by the pressure of the gag and she couldn't help him, so she just lay there, letting him do it all.

The gag almost made a sound like a plop or a sigh as he pulled the last of it out of her mouth. It was all matted, pushed together, firm, pulpy, very wet, almost foul, and he put it down on the bed because he didn't want to touch it any more.

A little shiver passed down his spine as he let go of the gag. After the act of sex was over, the whole bondage thing and its equipment disgusted him. He didn't want to have anything to do with it . . . until the next time.

She slowly closed her mouth as if she were performing a pleasure like eating a chocolate. Then her tongue came slowly out. It was delicate, pink, and it slowly licked her lips awkwardly as if it had never been used before.

She closed her eyes.

He untied her hands and she awkwardly withdrew them from behind her back and rested them on her hips. Her wrists were red and white with rope impressions. She lay there without moving. Her eyes were still closed. She licked her lips again.

Then her eyes opened slowly to see him staring at her.

"Come here, baby," she said.

Thirst

They lay cuddled around each other in bed, feeling very sad. They always felt sad after making love, but they felt sad most of the time, anyway, so it really didn't make that much difference, except that they were now warm and touching each other without any clothes on and passion, in its own particular way, had just crossed their bodies like a flight of strange birds or one dark bird flying.

They didn't say anything for a long time.

Constance, while she listened to the nighttime traffic like the ticking of a clock, thought about Bob and how much she loved him and wondered how much longer she could take things as they were now and why couldn't he get rid of the warts and why had two doctors failed in treating him.

She knew that everything had to have an ending.

Then she thought about a glass of water.

Bob was of course thinking about the *Greek Anthology*.

" *'Thou art exceedingly afraid,'* " he quoted in his mind.

"I'm thirsty," Constance said.

Locomotive Bubble

"OH, GOD! THE BOWLING TROPHIES ARE GONE!"

More on the
Greek Anthology

"Do you want to hear some more from the *Greek Anthology*?" Bob asked Constance. He was holding the book in his hands. It was a 1928 Putnam edition, a part of The Loeb Classical Library, with gold lettering on a dark cover. He had all three volumes of the *Greek Anthology*, but he could never find more than one book at a time. They kept disappearing and reappearing like mysteries in the house.

The pages of the book had been stained yellowish by time and the book had that dusty smell to it that can make some people feel sad for no apparent reason. Tattered window shades in old abandoned houses can have the same effect on certain people.

"Yes," she said. "That would be nice," but she really

didn't give a shit about the Greek Anthology. All she wanted was a glass of water.

"Let me go get a glass of water," she said. "I'm thirsty." She started to get out of bed.

"No, let me," Bob said. "Stay where you are."

He put the book down and got up from the bed and left the room. She had wanted to get the glass of water herself but before she could say anything he was gone. She was really thirsty and didn't want to trust it to his ineptness.

She wondered how long it would take him to get the glass of water, that is, if he could remember what he had gone to the kitchen for after he got there.

Constance was right.

Ten minutes passed before he came back.

The minutes passed slowly because she was very thirsty. She had been gagged for a long time that evening.

Constance looked at the book on the bed. She started to pick up the book but withdrew her hand just before it reached the book. She hated the Greek Anthology because it was a major part of the unhappiness that surrounded them. To her this book of ancient poetry was a symptom of the warts.

She had a sudden compulsion to throw the book out the window, watching it land down below in the evening traffic, but then she changed her mind instantly, while the book was still falling through the air in her mind.

She returned her thoughts to wondering what was keeping him in the kitchen. Normally, a glass of water was a simple matter. She felt sad again.

Ten minutes passed.

Constance started to get out of bed, then she heard Bob coming down the hall, so she stayed where she was and finished out the last seconds of the waiting.

"Here you are," Bob said, smiling. He had a sandwich in his hand. "A nice peanut butter sandwich with strawberry jam. This should take care of your hunger."

Bob handed Constance the sandwich.

She stared at it.

The Logan Brothers
Take Their Vows

A thunder and lightning storm came up out of nowhere on the night of the stolen bowling trophies. The Logan brothers stared at the empty cabinet with disbelieving eyes while above them the crack of bowling pin thunder and lightning, like a mad bowling ball, startled the sky.

The storm was a perfect 300 game.

Hatred took possession of the Logan brothers' blood as they stared at the empty cabinet. Whoever took the trophies did not even have the courtesy to leave one behind. What bastards they were!!! and now they had placed themselves outside the laws of man.

The Logan brothers swore vengeance.

Their mother held the family Bible in her hands as the Logan brothers grimly vowed to find the stolen bowling trophies and return them, no matter how long it took and what privations they suffered, to their rightful place: the oak cabinet in their parents' house.

The storm shook the house.

Their mother was crying as she held the Bible.

Their father stared down at the floor, wishing that he was working on a transmission.

The Logan sisters were of course elsewhere doing again together what they had done seven times before. If there were a category in the *Guinness Book of World Records* for what they were doing, they would have held the record.

Their father wished that life was as simple as transmissions.

Too bad.

A Typical
California Room
During the Decline
of the West

Fifty or so bowling trophies and a large papier-mâché bird can take up a lot of space in a room and that's what they did standing together in the front room of an apartment somewhere in San Francisco.

There were also two chairs and a couch, a phonograph and a television set that didn't work in the room, but Willard and his bowling trophies made them seem almost invisible as if the room were void of everything except Willard and the trophies.

You talk about personality.

Strangers would come into the room and say, "My God, what's that?" pointing at Willard and his bowling trophies.

"That's Willard and his bowling trophies," was always the reply.

"Willard and his what?"

"Bowling trophies."

"You mean bowling trophies?"

"Yeah, bowling trophies."

"What's he doing with them?"

"Why not?"

"I Know the Tunes
of All the Birds"

While Constance ate her peanut butter and strawberry jam sandwich, Bob read some more to her from the *Greek Anthology*, not knowing that she couldn't stand it, no matter how beautiful, poignant or wise the poetry was. To her it was only a shadow of the warts.

" 'I know the tunes of all the birds,' " he quoted, holding the book in his hands as they lay there naked upon the bed. They still hadn't put any clothes on yet. They both had handsome bodies.

"Isn't that beautiful?" he said. "That's all that's left of a poem. I wonder what happened to the rest of it. So many things can happen in two thousand years. Wars and, you know, all sorts of stuff like that. Plagues and countries and whole civilizations passing away. It must have been a beautiful poem."

Constance took a bite of her sandwich. She still hadn't had anything to drink yet and was just as thirsty as she had been before and here she was eating a peanut butter and strawberry jam sandwich.

She didn't know why she was eating the sandwich. Ever since he had brought her the sandwich instead of a glass of water, nothing seemed to make much difference.

"Do you like your sandwich?" Bob asked.

Constance nodded her head.

Telephone Answering Practice

The Logan brothers continued to wait in their little hotel room for the telephone to ring, the 3,000-dollar call that would tell them where the trophies were.

The comic-book-reading Logan had just finished with his book. He didn't know what else to do, so he just stared at the wallpaper for a while. He wished the telephone would ring. Then he got bored staring at the wallpaper and he went back to looking at the ads in the comic book. He paused again at the salve ad. It intrigued him.

The beer-drinking Logan brother had finished his beer. It was his last one and he wished that he had another one. He had become quite a beer drinker since the bowling trophies had been stolen. He wanted to go out for another beer but he didn't say anything about it. His brothers did not approve of him drinking beer all the time and he had been lucky to have the beer that he had just finished. They wanted him clearheaded when the telephone rang because they had some very serious business to do that evening.

The pacing Logan was now sitting on the bed beside his brother. He had become tired of pacing in the little room. He had also put the pistol away in a suitcase. He stared at the telephone. Soon it would ring and three long years of searching would be over. He opened and closed his right hand a few times. He did it in a way that his brothers could not see what he was doing. He was practicing how to answer the telephone.

The Search Begins

After the Logan brothers had taken their vows the evening of the stolen bowling trophies, they stayed around town for a month, looking for the bowling trophies but they couldn't find a single clue to their disappearance or whereabouts. They turned the town upside down but to no avail. It was as if the bowling trophies had vanished off the face of the earth.

They put a conspicuous advertisement in the local newspaper promising a large reward for the bowling trophies with no questions asked. The ad ended with the word PLEASE, but all they got were inconclusive telephone calls that led to nothing. They also received some crank calls.

"Hello, are you the people who put the ad in the

paper promising a reward for some stolen bowling trophies?"

"Yes, we are."

"Well, listen carefully. I'm the one who kidnapped the bowling trophies and I want 5,000 dollars ransom for them and you'd better not call the FBI or I'll melt the trophies down. Do you get that?"

"Who is this?" asked a bewildered Logan brother.

"Never mind who it is. Just keep listening. You'll be getting a note from me instructing you on what to do next. Remember, I want 5,000 dollars for the bowling trophies and don't call the FBI if you know what's good for you and the trophies."

"What?" the Logan brother answered. "Who is this?"

Then *click* . . .

They had hung up.

The note never came and the Logan brothers never heard from the person again.

Once they got a breather who sounded as if he were in the last stages of TB, a real death rattle.

hhhhhhhhhh (Cough

"Who is this?"

Middle Fork,
Colorado

A month after the bowling trophies had been stolen, the Logan brothers came to the conclusion that the bowling trophies had been taken some place else and they hadn't the slightest idea where, but it would be up to them to find out.

America was a very large place and the bowling trophies were very small in comparison.

The Logan brothers knew that they just couldn't sit around town, waiting for something to happen because it might not happen and they would never find the bowling trophies.

The trophies would be gone forever.

The Logan brothers started making plans to leave town. The Logan brothers had no idea where they were going but they had to go some place if they were ever going to find the trophies.

The day before they were going to leave, not knowing where they were going to go but anyplace would be a beginning, somebody called up on the telephone and told them that they thought the bowling trophies were in Middle Fork, Colorado.

The Logan brother who answered the telephone said thank you.

The brothers got a map and looked up Middle Fork, Colorado. The town was over a thousand miles away in the Rockies. They stared silently at the map for a long time.

Finally, one of the brothers spoke. "It's a beginning," he said.

Logan Farewell

The next morning they said good-bye to their mother and she cried a lot at the parting. They would have liked to have said good-bye to their sisters but they couldn't do that because their sisters were at that place again where they had been seven times before. By now, they must have set some kind of world record. The place was a hundred miles away in the opposite direction of where the bowling trophies might be, so . . . They would see their sisters at another time. Perhaps by then they would have recovered the bowling trophies and it would be a pleasant occasion and things would be like they used to be with the trophies in their cabinet again.

The Logan brothers had quit their jobs the day after the trophies had been stolen, so they could devote all their time to looking for them, a path that had led them only to frustration until they got the telephone call telling them that the trophies were in Middle Fork, Colorado.

The Logan brothers put three suitcases in the trunk of their car that had formerly transported many a just-won bowling trophy from the alleys to the cabinet. The car had once been full of happy Logan brothers. The Logan brothers that got into the car now were not the same boys they had been before.

They were all sitting in the front seat of the car because the back seat was filled with cakes, cookies and pies. The car drove slowly away. Their mother waved tearfully at them from the front porch of the only home they had ever known.

Their future was America and three long years of searching and a process of gradual character disintegration and a slow retreat from respectability and self-pride. In three years they would become what they had always despised.

They drove over to the garage where their father worked on transmissions. They didn't get out of the car because they were very anxious to get going.

Their father stood beside the car with a wrench in his hand. He didn't know what to say to them. He had a lot of trouble talking to people. Sometimes he wished that people were transmissions. Then he would be able to get along with them better. His sons looked very grim, sitting there. They had forgotten to shave that morning. They had always been very clean in their appearance and shaved every day before the bowling trophies had been stolen.

Since then their appearance had started downhill and

would continue to travel in that direction until they ended up looking very seedy and disrespectable, the kind of men that made honest people very nervous when they saw them.

"I guess you boys are going after the bowling trophies," their father said.

The brothers nodded.

"Well, good luck," their father said and walked back into the garage to a waiting transmission.

The Logan brothers drove off.

Greta Garbo
and Willard

Three years later in San Francisco, Patricia said to John after they had just come back from a movie, "Do you think Greta Garbo would like Willard?"

They were sitting on the couch, drinking glasses of cold white wine in the room where Willard reigned with his bowling trophies. Sometimes the expression on Willard's face was different. He looked slightly apprehensive now as if something were going to happen that he did not like.

The ability of Willard's face to change had something to do with the way the artist had created Willard after waking from his dream.

Willard was a kind of bird *Mona Lisa*.

"Maybe," John said. "You can't tell. Willard is an acquired taste."

"I think Greta Garbo would like Willard," Pat said.

Pat and John did not notice the look of apprehension on Willard's face. They were enjoying their wine and thinking about other things, so to them Willard was just good old Willard and his bowling trophies.

"How old is Greta Garbo?" John asked.

"I think she's sixty-eight," Pat said. "I may be wrong. She may be a little older or a little younger but she's somewhere in her sixties."

"How old is Willard?" John said.

"I don't know. Three or four years," Pat said.

"Don't you think Greta Garbo is a little old for Willard?" John said.

"No, I think they'd be good friends."

"Greta Garbo is a loner," John said. "Remember that. And Willard is very fond of his bowling trophies."

"That cannot be denied," Pat said.

The Game Is Over

"John and Pat are back from the movie," Constance said. She had finished her sandwich and was now getting dressed. Bob had stopped reading from the *Greek Anthology* and was sitting on the bed, watching her. He liked to watch her get dressed. He hadn't started to put any clothes on yet.

"How do you know?" he said.

"I can hear them moving around downstairs," Constance said.

Patricia and John always made a lot of noise when they first entered their apartment and the noise travelled up through the floor. The noise was very easy to hear. Bob just wasn't listening any more. Before he got the warts in his penis he used to complain about it all the time,

"They're nice people but why are they so God-damn noisy!" Now he didn't say anything about it.

"They went to see a Greta Garbo movie," Constance said, slipping a dress over her head. "They're big Greta Garbo fans."

"What?" Bob said.

"That was a good sandwich," Constance said.

"You look very pretty," Bob said.

She did, too.

"Thank you," Constance said and tossed her head, causing her long blonde hair to fall across her shoulder. She walked over to the dresser and got a brush and started to brush her hair in the mirror.

The dress had short sleeves. The rope marks were visible on her wrists. They were red and slightly weltish. They looked very incongruous.

Bob put his clothes on.

Then he picked up the ropes that were lying on the bed. He took the ropes and put them in a hall closet on a shelf. Actually, he was hiding them under a blanket that was on the shelf. He was ashamed of them but he could not stop himself from using them on her. He wished that things could be different but they weren't. They just stayed the same after the warts.

Maybe they would change next week.

He certainly hoped so.

Day after day, week after week, month after month, he had been hoping so.

He had forgotten the gag and went back into the bedroom to get it. Constance had finished brushing her hair. She turned to say something to Bob when he came back into the room but when she saw that he had returned to get the gag, she went back to brushing her hair in the mirror without saying what she was going to say.

He took the gag into the bathroom. He didn't like the way it felt in his hand. It was soaking wet with her spit. His ears started burning with embarrassment. He would be very glad when the gag wasn't in his hand any more. When he had taken the gag out of her mouth, it had been a warm wet but now it was a cold wet. That didn't make him feel very good either.

Bob put the gag in the dirty-clothes basket in the bathroom. Actually, he was hiding it among the dirty clothes, feeling shame again.

Then he washed his hands very carefully with soap as if he had fouled them with some kind of strange excrement. He washed his hands for a long time.

Constance left the bedroom and walked down the hall past the open door of the bathroom where he was standing there washing totally clean hands over and over again. He was so absorbed in washing his hands that he didn't notice her when she walked by.

She went into the kitchen and got a glass of water.

Bob dried his hands.

He went back to the bedroom to see Constance.

She wasn't there.

"Where are you?" he yelled down the hall.

"I'm here in the kitchen."

Salve

Finally the Logan brother couldn't take it any more. "I think I'll go out and get another beer," he said. "This waiting makes one thirsty. I'll be back in just a minute. There's a store open right on the corner." He started to stand up. He thought that he could fake his way out.

"No," said the Logan brother who had just a few seconds before been practicing how to answer the telephone when it rang and a strange voice told them where the bowling trophies were. He already knew what his first words would be after the person told him where the bowling trophies were. "If you're lying, you're dead," would be the words.

"Why not?" the beer-drinker Logan brother said. He said why not like a child would say it after he had been refused an ice-cream cone or something. There was a slight whine to the beer-drinker's voice. It sounded strange coming from him because he looked very mean . . . like a real outlaw.

"Because I say so," was his brother's reply. He was the older brother and was not given to explaining things after he had made a decision. Things were a closed matter when he said they were.

The beer-drinker started to say something that would have been a plea for beer but he knew that it would be useless, so he didn't say it. "I wish that fucking telephone would ring," was what he said instead and there was no child-like whine to it. This time his voice sounded the way he looked.

The comic-book-reading Logan didn't even bother to look up from the salve ad while this exchange went on. He wondered why he had never sold salve when he was a kid. It looked like a real interesting way to make money.

The Cows

Three years ago the bowling trophies were not in Colorado.

It had been a long drive for them across hundreds of miles of flatlands and then way up into the mountains until finally they arrived at a small town that had a population of 123 people. They went to the address that had been given to them over the telephone, but there was no street or house there, just a long field at the edge of town with some cows grazing on it.

The cows stopped eating to look at the Logan brothers.

The Downstairs Apartment

After talking about a possible friendship between Greta Garbo and Willard for a while and drinking a glass of wine, Patricia and John decided that it was time to go to bed, even though it was a little early. It was twenty after ten. They usually went to bed around midnight. John liked to watch a little bit of the Johnny Carson show on television. He said that it helped him sleep. It didn't make any difference at all to Patricia because she was sound asleep as soon as her head touched the pillow.

Patricia and John did not know that they were at odds when they decided to go to bed early.

He was tired and wanted to sleep.

She was not tired and wanted to make love.

They said good night to Willard and left the front room.

"Don't forget the bowling trophies," Pat said.

"Good night, bowling trophies," John said, *clicking* the light off and leaving Willard with his beloved bowling trophies, which was the way it was always meant to be.

It was not until they had taken off their clothes and gotten into bed that Patricia and John's differences in romantic attitudes were discovered.

Patricia cuddled around John and began touching him in ways that were different from a good-night kiss. John was very, *very* tired.

He tried to ignore her, hoping that she would get the message. She did not get the message. He rolled over to the other side of the bed. She followed him.

"I'm too tired," he said, finally.

"You can pretend I'm Greta Garbo," Pat said. "Would you like that? Pretend I'm Greta Garbo. Come on. I'm Greta Garbo and I want you," Pat whispered moistly into his ear.

"I'm still too tired," John said. "And that's nothing against Greta Garbo or you."

"Are you sure?" she said, touching his penis intriguingly with her hand.

"I'm sure," he said, brushing her hand away as if it were a mosquito.

Patricia gave up. She rolled over on her back and stared up at the darkened ceiling. "I wish Willard had a penis," she said.

"You're not his type," John said.

"What do you mean by that?" Patricia said, turning over to face his back.

"You're not a bowling trophy," John said.

93

The Sandwich

"Are you hungry?" Bob asked Constance.

She was sitting at the kitchen table, half-looking at a magazine.

"No," she said. "I just had a sandwich."

The Super Race

Patricia decided to try another time at seducing John. She would work on his sense of humor. Sometimes when he was in a funny mood, he would get horny. She didn't know why this was but she was not above using it. Patricia was twenty-five years old and very interested in sex. John was also very interested in sex but he was tired this evening.

"How do you know that I'm not a bowling trophy? Sometimes you treat me just like one," Patricia said in a very sexy voice which was breathing delicately on his back.

"What do you mean by that?" John said, sleepily.

"You know what I mean."

"No, I don't."

Patricia had slipped her hand like a warm shadow onto John's ass. It was barely there but he felt it.

"What are you doing?" he said. He was going to brush her hand away again but somehow he didn't quite get around to it.

"When you first met me why didn't you tell me then that you would end up treating me like a bowling trophy?" The husky warmness of her voice on his back caused a shiver to go down his spine. Also, he was smiling a little in the dark. She couldn't see him smiling, but she felt she was getting some place. All was not lost by a long shot.

"I've never treated you like a bowling trophy," John said.

"Prove it, big boy," Patricia said, her hand slipping delicately over his ass and down toward his crotch.

"Don't do that," John said, but he didn't try to stop her.

"Make me, big boy," she said. Her voice felt like honey on his back while her hand, paying no attention, continued on its merry way.

"I'm sleepy," he said, smiling in the dark. "Have mercy."

"Bowling trophies know no mercy," she said, her hand arriving at its destination.

His smile had now become an invisible grin.

"What about Willard?" John said. "He'll be jealous."

"Are you going to tell him?"

"No," John said, with a big grin on his face.

"Well," Patricia said. "If you don't tell him neither will I and what Willard doesn't know won't hurt him."

"But what if Willard does find out? What then?" John said.

"We'll cross that bridge when we come to it," Patricia said.

"You're pretty sure of yourself," John said.

"We bowling trophies are a super race," Patricia said. "Haven't you noticed that yet?"

Some Salve Talk

Tension and boredom dominated the sleazy little hotel room the Logan brothers waited in. They hadn't said anything to each other in a long time. They just sat there. The frustrated beer-drinker Logan was feeling sorry for himself. Why couldn't he have just one more beer? What difference did it make? If the bowling trophies had never been stolen then he wouldn't have to sit here in this Goddamn hotel room without a beer.

His older brother who had denied him the beer request now had his hand on the table beside the telephone. He alternately stared at his right hand and then at the telephone.

The comic-book-reading Logan was still fascinated by the salve ad. "Hey," he said, looking up from the comic book to his brothers.

"What is it?" the denied beer-drinker Logan brother said.

"Yeah, what do you want?" the one beside the telephone said.

"Why didn't we ever sell salve when we were kids?"

"What kind of salve?" the telephone Logan said.

"You know, for cuts and burns. Salve."

"Where were we going to get this salve and who was going to buy it?" the telephone Logan said. He was really looking at his brother now, who was sitting up on the bed with an open comic book in his lap.

"We'd get it from the comic book here and sell it around the neighborhood to people."

The beer-drinker Logan brother wanted a beer now more than ever. He smacked his lips. He could taste an imaginary beer in his mouth.

"What if they didn't want to buy any salve? What would we do with the salve, then?" the telephone Logan said.

"It says here in the comic book that people want to buy salve. A lot of people." He tried to show a picture in the comic book of people buying salve to his brother.

"That comic book is full of shit," the telephone Logan said, paying no attention to the picture of people buying salve. "People don't buy salve from kids. They buy it at the drugstore. Would you buy salve from some dumb kid if you had a burn? No, you'd go down to the drugstore. That's where you get salve."

"It says here—" the comic-book-reading Logan said, still persisting. He had done a lot of thinking about the salve ad.

"You don't even know what's in that salve. Do you? Come on, do you?"

"No, but—"

RRRRRRRRRRIIIIIIIIIIINNNNNNNNNNGGGGGGGGGG

The telephone rang.

!!!

"Fallen Upon
Evil Times"

"Well, if you're not hungry, I think I'll have something to eat," Bob said. "I'm really hungry. I don't know why."

"Maybe you're just hungry," Constance said.

"That's it," Bob said. "That's it all right."

He looked over at Constance sitting at the kitchen table. Then he looked away. He didn't like to see the rope marks on her wrists.

"I think I'll see what's in the refrigerator," Bob said.

"That's a good idea," Constance said, without thinking.

Bob opened the refrigerator door and looked inside. After while Constance noticed that he was still standing there with the door open, looking inside, and she knew that he had forgotten what he was doing, that he was hungry and looking for something to eat in the refrigerator, so she gently reminded him.

"Do you see anything in there you want to eat?"

Her words startled him.

He had totally forgotten why he was there.

He saw some spaghetti sauce.

"I think I'll heat up this spaghetti sauce," he said, taking a bowl of spaghetti sauce out of the refrigerator and then closing the door.

She watched to make sure that he got the spaghetti sauce out of the bowl and into a pan and onto the stove and that he also remembered to turn the gas burner on. When she made sure that he had done all of these things, she got up from the table and started out of the kitchen.

"Where are you going?" he said.

"Into the front room," she said. "I think I'll put some music on the phonograph. Anything you want to listen to?"

"No," he said. "Play whatever you want. I'll just listen to whatever's playing."

"OK."

Constance went into the front room.

They had a large friendly-looking apartment that was cheerfully and creatively decorated with comfortable furniture and many well-taken-care-of plants.

From looking at their place there was no way of knowing the things that went on in the bedroom: his awkward sadism. It was a very feminine, healthy-looking room because Constance had done most of the work on it. One would never have known that there were ropes hidden on hall closet shelves under blankets and that in the bedroom

102

beautiful handkerchiefs and scarfs served the purpose of incompetent gags.

Also, hidden in the bedroom were bottles of medicine that he used to treat the warts in his penis, the warts that never went away. He had the bottles hidden in a box in the closet. There was stuff piled on top of the box as if it contained something the police were looking for.

Then there were of course the rubbers hidden under his socks in the dresser, the rubbers that he hated to buy, that always made him feel sick inside when he bought them, his ears burning with embarrassment and he never could look the person who sold him the rubbers in the eye. He always looked away.

He would check the drugstore out first to make sure that he would not have to buy the rubbers from a female clerk. He would only buy them from men. Bob even went so far as to make sure that there were no women in the store when he bought them. The rubbers were a descent into obscenity for him.

Bob watched his spaghetti sauce heat up. Red bubbles came slowly to the surface. He wondered what Constance was doing in the front room.

Their kitchen was large and friendly and filled with green growing things. He, she, they loved together green growing things.

Then he heard some music coming from the front room.

Bach.

Bob liked Bach.

It was nice of Constance to put something on the phonograph.

He waited for Constance to return to the kitchen. She didn't come back, so he stirred the spaghetti sauce.

Yes, there was no way of knowing what was going on in that house. Nobody knew. Though he'd had the warts for almost a year now, he'd told nobody about them, not even his best friends.

The warts were his exile and his dungeon.

His friends worried about him because he was a nice guy. They were also disturbed by him endlessly reading to them from the *Greek Anthology*.

The Logan Statues

RRRRRRRRIIIIIIIINNNNNNNNGGGGGGGG
!!!!!!
RRRRRRRRIIIIIIIINNNNNNNNGGGGGGGG
!!!!!!
RRRRRRRRIIIIIIIINNNNNNNNGGGGGGGG
!!!!!!
RRRRRRRRIIIIIIIINNNNNNNNGGGGGGGG
!!!!!!

The Logan brothers sat there staring at the telephone. Not one of them moved an inch. They were statues of Logan brothers. Now that the telephone was finally ringing after all of these years, they didn't know what to do.

The Logan who had done all of the telephone answering practice was the most helpless of all. His hand rested like marble beside the telephone.

RRRRRRRRIIIIIIIINNNNNNNNGGGGGGGG
!!!!!!
RRRRRRRRIIIIIIIINNNNNNNNGGGGGGGG
!!!!!!
RRRRRRRRIIIIIIIINNNNNNNNGGGGGGGG
!!!!!!
RRRRRRRRIIIIIIIINNNNNNNNGGGGGGGG
!!!!!!

Spaghetti

Bob was eating when Constance came back into the kitchen. She had been gone for about ten minutes. He had poured the sauce over a couple slices of bread. "Where were you?" he said.

"I was in the front room," she said.

"Oh," he said.

There was a green container of Kraft Parmesan cheese on the table beside his plate, but there was no cheese on his spaghetti sauce bread. He had forgotten to use it.

He felt a little better looking at Constance now because the rope marks on her wrists were gone. Now he wouldn't look away in embarrassment when she was around him.

She went over to the stove and put some water on for tea.

"What are you doing?" he asked.

"I'm putting some water on for tea," Constance said. "I feel like a cup of tea."

"That sounds good," he said, eating a bite of red bread.

She went over to the table and sat down in a chair beside him. "You look tired," she said, softly.

"That's funny. I don't feel tired," Bob said.

How would you know? Constance thought. *How would you ever know?*

Matthew Brady

Patricia and John were busy making immortal love in the bedroom. She had really turned John on by pretending to be a bowling trophy. After while she had gotten him laughing and for some reason or another sometimes it sexually aroused him and they were really going at love now.

Unbeknownst to them the ghost of Matthew Brady slipped supernaturally into the house and took a photograph of Willard and his bowling trophies. Matthew Brady posed them in such a way that Willard looked like Abraham Lincoln and the bowling trophies looked like his generals during the Civil War. There was a battlefield nearby but you couldn't see it.

Willard was very serious in the photograph and so

were the bowling trophies. They all played out their parts perfectly.

Matthew Brady left the apartment just about the time Patricia and John finished making famous love in the bedroom. They never saw him.

He disappeared back into the swirls of ghostly time, taking with him a photographic impression of Willard and his bowling trophies to be joined visually with the rest of American history because it is very important for Willard and his bowling trophies to be a part of everything that has ever happened to this land of America.

Marble to Flesh

The marble hand of the Logan brother beside the telephone suddenly became living flesh and he picked up the
telephone.

"Hello," he said.

The other two brothers stared at the sound of the
word hello as if it were a bolt of lightning in the air.

"NO!" he said, his face instantaneously flushing with
anger. "This is not Jack's Bar and Grill and I'm not Jack,
you son-of-a-bitch. YOU BASTARD!" He started banging
the receiver of the telephone on the table and the table fell
over and the telephone made a huge ringing noise when it
hit the floor.

The Logan brother was still sitting there, shouting,
"BASTARD! BASTARD!" at the receiver in his hand.

He was making a lot of noise because he had just gone mad.

The other two Logan brothers threw themselves on him and held him down on the bed until he came to his senses. The comic-book-reading Logan hung up the telephone. Obviously, it was a wrong number. The person was still on the other end of the line, "Hello, Jack? Is that you, Jack? Don't be mad, Jack. I'll pay you back the five I owe you, Jack. Jack? Are you there, Jack? It's only five—"

click

Three Long
Years Ago

The cows stopped eating to look at the Logan brothers.

Now one of them was stark raving mad in a cheap hotel room in San Francisco. His two brothers held him on the bed, trying to quiet him down.

"What are we going to do now?" one of the Logan brothers said, staring back at a cow.

It was just spring in Colorado and the day, though warm, had a slight crispness to it. The sky was clear and blue. The little town of Middle Fork was in a small valley and mountains towered up around it.

"I don't know," was one reply.

"Find the bowling trophies," was the other reply. It was a very stern reply. It had come from the brother *who was now being held down on the bed until he came to his senses.*

"Where do we look?" said the Logan who had started the conversation. He was the brother who liked to read comic books. He was still staring at the cow. He was staring at the cow in the same way that he read comic books.

"It doesn't make much difference where we look," his stern brother answered, surrounded by America in every direction. "Just as long as we keep looking until we find the trophies."

Finally, he was quiet on the bed in the hotel room. He was very quiet. "I'm OK," he said, in a slow calm voice. "It's all right now."

Spaghetti Bread Tears

A forkful of spaghetti bread was halfway to Bob's mouth moving along at a regular eating motion. One does not know how many miles per hour a fork travels when you are eating but his fork was moving at a normal speed when suddenly it slammed on its brakes in his hand and came to a screeching halt halfway to Bob's mouth.

Tears slowly started ebbing from his eyes and flowing down his cheeks. He had started crying. The tears became low slow sobbing while the fork remained halfway to his mouth with a bite of spaghetti bread resting precariously upon it.

"What is it?" Constance said, reaching over and taking the fork from Bob's hand and putting it down on the plate in front of him.

"What's wrong, honey?"

He didn't say anything.

He just sat there continuing to cry.

Constance reached over and took his hand in her hand. "What is it, baby? Tell me what it is."

Bob just kept crying.

Constance didn't try to find out any more from him why he was crying. She continued holding his hand but she left him alone in his sorrow.

The plate of spaghetti bread looked silly in front of a grown man crying. Constance didn't like to sit there holding his hand as he cried with that plate of stuff in front of them. It hurt her dignity and put Bob in a bad light, too.

She gently let go of Bob's hand and reached over and picked up the plate of spaghetti bread and got up and took it over to the sink.

Then she returned to Bob's hand again.

He cried for ten minutes.

Constance didn't say anything more.

She waited for Bob to stop crying.

Kansas

The Logan brothers spent that night in Middle Fork nosing around but they couldn't find any clues to why the house that the bowling trophies were supposed to be in wasn't there.

Besides that, people looked at them as if they were a little crazy. "That's a pasture out there," an old-timer said to them, looking at them very carefully in the town bar. They waited for him to say something else about the pasture but that was it. The Logan brothers felt a little uncomfortable. They said thank you and tried to find somebody else who could help them.

The old man told the story many times about the three strangers asking if there was a house out there and he said, " 'No, that's a pasture out there,' and then you know what they said to me? They said thank you for me telling them what they had seen with their very own eyes."

The old man always laughed when he finished telling the story about the three strangers who came into town looking for a house that was a pasture. "Yeah, they thanked me for telling them that," and whomever he'd told the story to would laugh along with him.

"I just don't know what the world's coming to," would be the final period at the end of the story.

The next day the Logan brothers left for Kansas. They had no reason to believe that the bowling trophies were in Kansas but they had to look some place and Kansas was just as good as any other place.

The Matthew Brady
Echo

Patricia and John were lying quietly beside each other in bed. They were very contented from their lovemaking. John had forgotten that he was tired and Patricia's mind was drained of all passion like an empty swimming pool in the winter.

"Did you hear something in the other room?" Patricia said finally, after a long peaceful time.

"No," John said. "I didn't hear anything."

"I thought I heard something," Patricia said.

"Well, I didn't hear anything," John said. "What did you hear? What did it sound like?"

"I don't know," she said.

John reached over and touched Patricia's hair. It felt beautiful in the dark.

"Maybe it was your imagination," he said.

A Change of Plans

After the brief violent outburst from the oldest Logan brother, the little hotel room had been returned to normal and the Logan brothers had gone back to waiting again for the telephone to ring and a voice to tell them where the bowling trophies were.

The Logan brother who had lost his cool wasn't sitting by the telephone any more. He had changed places on the bed with the comic-book-reading Logan who'd forgotten his comic book when they moved.

He was going to ask his brother to hand him the comic book but his brother was reading it now and he felt that it was better not to disturb him.

The comic-book-reading Logan had hurt his wrist in the wrestling match with his totally berserk brother and he thought that it was best just to let things be and for his brother to read the comic book in his stead.

The beer-drinker Logan still wanted a beer but he knew he wouldn't get one until the evening's activities were over and so . . . he felt sort of hopeless.

The telephone Logan who was now the comic-book-reading Logan was absent-mindedly staring at the same salve ad that he had put his brother down for reading a little while ago, but he really didn't see the ad. It was just color and motion in his hands. He was actually thinking about the bowling trophies and the people who had stolen them. He was thinking very hard and very grimly about them.

Then he looked up from the comic book to the telephone. The telephone was not ringing. It was just a strange black silent object on a table.

"Let's kill them," he said.

"What?" the brother by the telephone said.

"I said, let's kill them."

"Kill who?"

"You know who. The bastards who stole our bowling trophies. They don't deserve to live. Look what they've done to us. They've made us into animals. We're just animals now. Fucking animals."

"You mean, you want to kill them?"

"That's right."

"What do you think?" the one by the telephone asked the Logan who didn't have a beer in his hand but wanted one to be there and not having a beer in his hand suddenly made him very mad.

"Sure," he said. "Let's kill them."

121

If he'd had a beer, cold and comfortable, in his hand he would not have wanted to kill them. He would have said instead, "No, let's just beat the shit out of them and get our trophies and go home."

But because he didn't have a can of beer in his hand, he said, "Sure, let's kill them."

Now two Logan brothers were staring at the Logan brother who was sitting beside the telephone but would have preferred to be a child, selling salve to his neighbors and earning lots of money selling something that made people feel better when they used it and afterwards thought kindly of him for selling the salve to them.

"OK," he said, because he always did what his brothers did.

"Then it's settled," the Logan with the comic book on his lap said.

"Are you reading that comic book?" his brother asked him.

"No."

"Then can I read it?"

"Sure." His brother handed him the comic book and he immediately turned to the salve ad. Before he lost himself in the ad again, he thought for a moment about killing the people who'd stolen the bowling trophies. He'd never killed anybody before. He turned the comic book a few pages to some characters in the comic book who were killing each other. They were using axes and it was very bloody. A hand was lying on the floor. The hand did not look happy.

He looked up from the comic book to his brother on the bed. "How are we going to kill them?" he asked.

"We'll shoot them."

"Good," he said, and turned from the people in the comic book with the axes back to the salve ad. He liked the people in the salve ad because they were happy selling salve.

In his mind he pressed a doorbell.

It rang pleasantly and somebody came to the door. It was an older man. The man looked like his grandfather except that he had red hair.

"Hello," the man said. "What can I do for you?"

"My name is Johnny Logan and I'm selling salve."

"Come on in, Johnny. It's hot out there. I'll get you a big glass of lemonade and then you tell me all about this salve. And if it sounds like good stuff, I'll buy a couple of tubes of it, and give you the names and addresses of some friends of mine who live nearby and might be interested in some salve."

"We'll shoot them in the heart," his brother said.

"That's good," he said, without looking up from the comic book.

"Here's your lemonade, son. Now tell me what kind of salve you've got here. If it's good salve, I don't care how much it costs."

"This is the best salve in the world. It's made in Chicago, Illinois."

"Right in the fucking heart."

"These Things Began,
'Tis Said,
with Our Fathers"

"I'm crying because of all those Greeks," Bob said.

His face was so full of tears that there wasn't room for another tear. He tried to find enough room for one more tear but he couldn't find it, so he stopped crying.

"What Greeks?" Constance said and as the words left her mouth, she knew what Greeks. It was *those* Greeks. She wished that she hadn't asked the question.

"The ones in the *Greek Anthology*," Bob said.

"What about them?" Constance said and then realized that she'd said it. She felt as if she'd subconsciously set a trap for herself and then fallen into it.

"They're dead," Bob said.

Two Kitchens

John and Patricia decided that they wanted a little snack before they went to sleep. It was close to midnight and their normal bedtimes. They were hungry from the sexual exercise they had just gone through.

"What time is it?" John said.

Patricia looked at the clock beside the bed because John couldn't see it from where he was lying in the bed.

"It's almost twelve," she said.

"Well, let's go get a snack and come back here and eat it in bed while I watch a little of the Johnny Carson show," John said.

"Everything's back to normal," Patricia said, jumping out of bed and wiggling her ass at John.

"HHHHHHHHEEEEEEEEERRRRRRRRREEEEEEEE"""" SSSSSSSS, Johnny!"

"You don't have to watch him if you don't want to," John said.

"I'm going to dance with Willard instead," Patricia said. "He knows how to show a girl a good time. He does a great two-step."

She started dancing around the room, pretending that she was holding Willard in her arms. She acted as if she were dodging something with her head. "Watch out for your beak, Willard," she said.

John went into the kitchen. He didn't bother to put any clothes on. He was hungry. Patricia joined him a moment later. She didn't have any clothes on either: not a stitch. Her body was quite adequate. John was a little overweight. He had a slight potbelly, but he didn't give a damn. His whole family ran toward being a little overweight and so he was used to it and considered that he was carrying on a family tradition by having a potbelly.

He was thirty-one years old.

Patricia was six years younger.

They got along very well together and had been doing so for almost five years. He was a filmmaker and she was a school teacher.

He worked with visions and she taught Spanish.

They were pleased with what they did with their lives.

Patricia and John's kitchen was directly underneath Bob and Constance's kitchen and they were at this moment all in their own kitchens.

Upstairs Bob was mourning people who had been dead for over two thousand years. Constance was trying to console him. Tears were slowly drying on his face.

Downstairs John was making a turkey sandwich. He was pulling off pieces of meat from an ornate-looking turkey carcass on the table.

Patricia was pouring out big glasses of ice-cold milk to go with the sandwiches while they watched the Johnny Carson show in the bedroom, and as soon as she finished with her sandwich and glass of milk, she would be fast asleep and John would stay up with Johnny Carson for a little while and then he would join her in sleep.

"Lots of white meat on mine," Patricia said. "And don't short me on the mayonnaise."

"Have I ever done that to you?" John said.

"No, but there's always a first time for everything."

"Jesus," he said at exactly the same time that upstairs in the kitchen above them, Bob said, "I don't want to cry any more for dead people."

Constance tried to think of something to console him but she couldn't think of anything, so she remained silent, sitting beside him at the table, holding his hand.

Of course Bob and Constance couldn't hear what Patricia and John were saying downstairs and neither of the couples knew what the other couple was doing.

That's one of the strange things about people living in apartment buildings. They barely know what anybody else is doing. The doors are made out of mystery.

"More mayonnaise and more pepper," Patricia said.

"Don't think about it any more," Constance said.

A Visit to Kansas

The Logan brothers spent six months in Kansas looking for the stolen bowling trophies. They looked very carefully in Topeka, Dodge City, Wichita, Kansas City, etc.,
etc., etc., etc.,
cities, cities of Kansas:
Reserve,
Ulysses,
Pretty Prairie,
and Gas, Kansas.

They looked in the windows of houses in quiet residential neighborhoods. Maybe the person who stole the trophies was a show-off and wanted people to see the trophies in his front window like a Christmas tree.

They looked under bridges and in wheat fields.

They hung around bowling alleys, deliberately over-
hearing conversations, hoping that they might find a clue
in listening to bowlers talking to each other. Maybe one of
them would spill the beans but it all came to nothing.

The Logan brothers spent the money that they had
taken with them when they left home and they didn't
want to get jobs because that would take away valuable
time from looking for the bowling trophies.

So they became minor thieves: shoplifting, breaking
into parked cars, newspaper-rack coin boxes, etc. One
night in Pretty Prairie they stole a rug off the clothesline
in somebody's backyard and stepped in a bed of flowers.

"Watch out for the flowers."

"Oh, shit! I stepped on them."

"Big feet!"

That's the kind of stuff the Logan brothers were
doing.

Before the bowling trophies were stolen, they had
never engaged in activities like this. They were honest
and looked up to as heroes, and all the mothers in town
wanted their sons to grow up and be like the Logan
brothers and be champion bowlers.

Toward
an Understanding
of Television
and Sleep

Patricia and John nakedly took big turkey sandwiches and glasses of ice-cold milk into the bedroom. They were doing a very good imitation of American health.

John turned the television set on and Johnny Carson popped into the room, like a firecracker on the TV screen. He had just finished telling a joke and everybody was laughing except the guest sitting next to him. The guest was not laughing. The guest looked very dour.

Ed McMahon, Carson's cohort, then said something and the guest smiled and Johnny Carson brought up a subject that really interested the guest.

The subject was the guest and the guest immediately started talking about the guest and then everything was running smoothly. John liked to watch this kind of stuff before he went to sleep. It helped him sleep better. He used to have a little trouble falling asleep but the Johnny Carson show had changed that. After twenty or thirty minutes of the Johnny Carson show, he was ready to sleep like a babe.

"We have three turkey sandwiches," Patricia said.

"What do you mean?" John said.

Patricia motioned her head toward the TV set. She didn't like television very much. She had never had any problem sleeping at night, so she just didn't understand.

Dust

All of Bob's tears were dry now and turning to dust on his cheeks. It was a little after midnight. He and Constance were totally exhausted. There wasn't a single emotion left for them to feel.

"Let's go for a walk," Bob said.

"All right," Constance said.

They got up from the kitchen table and went into the hall. Constance was going to turn the light out as she left the kitchen, but then she thought: *What difference does it make?*

None.

They got their coats out of the closet.

When they left the apartment, Bob tried to lock the front door but he wasn't able to do it right the first time he tried, so he had to lock the door a second time before he actually got it locked.

All of the lights in the apartment were on.

And Constance didn't care.

Finally Something
to Replace
Bowling

The Logan brothers held up their first filling station in New Mexico. They had left Kansas three weeks before. The only reason they were in New Mexico was because of the bowling trophies. They had gone to New Mexico for the same reason they had gone to Kansas because they had to go some place and one place was just as good as another if you're looking for stolen bowling trophies in America and you haven't the slightest idea where they're at.

The station was just outside of Albuquerque.

They needed some money and they were tired of stealing little things. It took too much time. It took as much energy to steal six little things as it took to steal one medium thing: like holding up a filling station, which would also give them the opportunity to get a tank of gas in the bargain.

So one day in Albuquerque the Logans talked it over and decided to go into the business of holding up filling stations. And the fact that they could get free gas by doing this weighed heavily in their decision.

While they were talking it over, one of the brothers said, "I'm tired of stealing rugs."

The other brothers agreed.

"I'm also very tired of stealing newspaper racks."

The other brothers told him that they would never do anything like that again.

The filling station was on the edge of Albuquerque. It only had one attendant. He was an old man who was tired of pumping gas. It was toward the end of his shift and he looked forward to going home and drinking some beer and watching television.

He'd had it for that day.

Pooped.

The Logan brothers drove into the station and told the attendant to fill it up.

"Regular or ethyl?"

"Ethyl," one of the brothers said.

Normally, they ordered regular. It was going to be ethyl from now on out for the Logan brothers.

"Check the oil, too," one of them said.

The attendant checked the oil while the tank was being filled with gas. He took a careful look at the dip stick. He had to because he needed glasses but he wouldn't get them because he was too vain. He'd been quite a ladies' man in his youth but you couldn't tell it by looking at him now. He just looked like any other old man you'd see on the street.

"It's down two quarts," he said.

"Put some in," a Logan brother said. "30 weight. Your best."

"OK," the old man said, and tiredly went and got the oil.

After the car was filled with gas and oil, the old man informed the Logan brothers that the cost for these items would be $11.75.

"Cash or credit?" he said.

"Neither," one of them said, getting out of the car. The Logan brother did not have a gun but he had something bulging in his coat pocket that simulated one.

"This is a stickup." He liked it when he said that. It sounded exactly like something a gangster would say in a movie. Maybe that's where he'd heard it and he was just repeating it but he didn't care because it made him feel good saying it.

"Just don't hurt me," the old man said, staring at the gun-like bulging thing that was pointing at him from the pocket of the standing Logan. He didn't know that it was a rolled-up comic book.

"We won't hurt you if you pay attention. All we want is your money. If you don't want to pay attention and give us your life, too, that's your business."

The Logan brother was really enjoying saying these things. Why hadn't they done this in the first place instead of stealing cans of tuna fish from the grocery stores?

This was the way to do it!

The old man gave them the money. It was a hundred

and seventy-two dollars and thirty-five cents. The Logan brothers hadn't seen that much money in months.

"You promised you wouldn't hurt me."

"Have we hurt you yet?"

"No."

"Did you pay attention?"

"I think so. Yes. Yes, I did. I gave you the money."

"Come on," one of the Logan brothers said from the car. "Let's get out of here." He was getting tired of listening to his brother pretend to be a gangster.

"You lived up to your part of the bargain and we'll live up to ours. We're that kind of men."

"For Christ's sake!" came the voice of a Logan from the car. He was starting to get a little sick at his stomach. He couldn't believe that his brother was going through this routine.

"All right," his brother said, getting back into the car. "We always keep our word!" he shouted at the trembling-old-man-filling-station attendant.

It was two hours and halfway to Gallup, New Mexico, before his brothers would talk to him.

"What did I do? Tell me. Come on. What's wrong?"

But they wouldn't answer him, even though he kept pestering them. Finally, one of them said something. He said, "You're an idiot! That's what."

After his brother said that to him, he didn't say anything for a while. He just stared sullenly out the window, thinking about why *one of them* didn't get out of the car with a comic book rolled up in his pocket and hold up the old man if they were such hot shit.

The Five-Gallon
Gang

The next Logan brothers' filling station holdup was a lot easier. They didn't use a comic book for a gun this time. They took some of the money from the first filling station holdup and bought a .22 revolver but they didn't get any bullets for the gun. It was not until their 4th filling station holdup that they got some bullets for the gun and it wasn't until their 32nd filling station holdup that they used the gun to shoot an attendant in the leg and it wasn't until their 67th filling station holdup that they shot an attendant right between the eyes, bringing an abrupt and eternal halt to his pumping gas.

The second filling station holdup was done in a lot less dramatic fashion than the first one. It did not employ any late-show 1930's gangster histrionics in its execution.

It started off like this:

very low keyed,

"This is a holdup,"

etc.

The Logan brothers just simply held up the filling station. They were becoming polished professional filling station holdup men in a very short time. You might even say that they were precocious about holding up filling stations and soon they were able to do it with the same efficiency that they had previously dedicated to bowling.

During the 5th filling station holdup they started using an MO that the police identified them with and the newspapers built up into an image.

The Logan brothers did their usual thing of having the tank filled and the oil checked before they announced their intentions to the attendant but then while the robbery was being executed, one of the brothers took a five-gallon can from the trunk and filled it up with gas.

One evening just before this particular robbery, they decided that they needed every drop of gasoline that they could get their hands on to find the stolen bowling trophies and why not get an extra can of gas as part of the robberies.

"Sounds like a good idea," one of the Logan brothers said.

The other two agreed.

And the newspapers referred to them after that as the "Five-Gallon Gang."

FIVE-GALLON GANG STRIKES IN FLAGSTAFF
LAST SEEN DRIVING TOWARD PRESCOTT
BUT VANISH INTO THIN AIR
POLICE CAN'T FIND THEM

No, these were not the simple honest Logan brothers who'd left home less than a year ago in search of their stolen bowling trophies.

"Why did you kill him?"

"Do you want to go back to stealing rugs out of back-yards and stepping all over people's flowers?"

"No, but I don't think you should have killed him. He wasn't doing anything. He was just getting the money like all the rest of the guys except for that guy we had to shoot in the leg. He was bothersome, so we had to shoot him. He was a son-of-a-bitch and I'd shoot him again if I had the chance, but I wouldn't kill him."

"Then you *do* want to go back to stealing rugs?"

"No!"

The Logan brother who wasn't in the conversation was drinking a can of beer. They tried to get him into the conversation.

"What do you think?"

He didn't answer. He just waved his can of beer in such a way as to show that he wasn't interested. He had no interest. All he wanted to do was enjoy cold beer trickling down his throat.

Johnny Carson

Patricia finished her turkey sandwich before John finished his. She wasn't a fast eater either. It was just that he was a very slow eater.

Constance was holding Bob's hand as they took a short walk to Fillmore Street. They didn't say anything as they walked along. The evening was still warm. They walked very slowly. When they reached Fillmore, they turned around and started walking back. They still hadn't said anything.

Patricia was asleep before John finished his sandwich. He continued eating his sandwich very, very slowly and watching Johnny Carson tell jokes. He tried not to laugh too hard at Johnny Carson's jokes because he didn't want to spit a mouthful of turkey sandwich all over the bed.

The next guest on the Johnny Carson show was a young actress who was wearing a dress with a very low neckline. She had giant breasts and tried to walk demurely over from the curtain to where Johnny Carson was sitting with his other guests. Johnny Carson made a joke about her breasts as she walked toward him. The audience laughed heartily. The actress tried to smile. And John spit a big mouthful of turkey sandwich all over the bed.

The actress sat down.

John checked to see if he had awakened Patricia when he laughingly spit the sandwich on the bed. No, he hadn't awakened her. Good. He didn't want her to see the pieces of turkey sandwich on the bed. That would have embarrassed him. He quickly cleaned them up.

The actress told Johnny Carson and millions of insomniac Americans, many of them surrounded by fragments of food that they had just laughed out of their mouths, that she had just finished making a Western in Italy.

That's all she said.

But Johnny Carson was able to use it to make another joke about her breasts. The audience laughed heartily again. John was glad that he didn't have any more food in his mouth.

Beards

The Logan who had gone berserk a little while before, and then after he'd come to his senses was able to convince his brothers that they should kill the people who had stolen the bowling trophies, had gotten the .22 pistol out of their only suitcase.

They'd had three suitcases when they started out looking for the bowling trophies but the Logans after a little while stopped paying any attention to their wardrobe any more and wore the same clothes all the time now. They didn't need three suitcases, so they carried their lives around in one battered suitcase.

It had been years since they'd brushed their teeth.

And they were very remiss in shaving but somehow they managed to shave just short of having beards on their

143

faces. They had considered wearing beards at one time, but they figured that it would make it too easy for the police to identify them. They didn't want that to happen because they knew that there was no way they were going to be able to find the bowling trophies if they were in prison.

One of the Logan brothers summed it up when he said, "No beards."

Cookies and
Cakes and
Pies
(Tons of

Though her beloved sons had been gone for three years without a word from them, Mother Logan continued baking just as many cakes and pies and cookies as she did when they were living there in the house.

Sometimes it was hard to find your way around the kitchen because it was so filled with baked stuff. Once Mr. Logan put a cup of coffee down in the kitchen and he couldn't find it among all that baking.

Mr. Logan had thought about asking his wife not to bake so much but he never got around to asking her. It was easier for him to live with all those cakes and pies and cookies than it was for him to say anything to anybody about anything.

If his wife were a transmission there would be a lot less cookies and pies and cakes in the house.

He never did find that cup of coffee.

A Vision
of Ringing

The older Logan brother took the pistol out of the suit-case. He opened the cylinder to make sure the gun was loaded. It was. The six little bullets rested in their six little homes. They were hollow points. They would tear a nice hole in you and provide you with enough death to last forever.

He flipped the cylinder back into the gun and then a few seconds later he opened the cylinder and looked at the bullets again. If more than six people had stolen the trophies, he'd beat the extra ones to death with the butt of the pistol.

He would prefer that there were six or less bowling trophy thieves because it was easier to shoot people than it was to beat them to death, but he wouldn't think twice about beating them to death if there happened to be more than six bowling trophy thieves.

"It's going to ring," the comic-book-reading Logan brother said, suddenly looking up from the salve ad to the telephone.

The beer drinker turned his head toward him.

The Logan brother with the gun in his hand looked over toward him.

The Logan brother who'd just said, "It's going to ring," started slowly to reach for the telephone, even though it was not ringing. It was just an ordinary silent black telephone, but he was reaching for it, anyway.

His two brothers watched him.

They wondered what he was doing.

The Logans
Unemployed

Three years is a long time to wander around America, looking for stolen bowling trophies. It can change a person. Sometimes for the worst, as was the case with the Logan brothers.

After they did not find the bowling trophies in New Mexico, though they had found a new occupation, they tried Arizona without a favorable conclusion to their searching.

Then they went to Connecticut and spent a month there: no bowling trophies. After that they went to Oklahoma and spent six months there and it was the same: no bowling trophies. They had by this time held up over a hundred filling stations.

They went to Louisiana, no luck there, and Indiana,

same story, but in Alabama they got a tip that the bowling trophies were in Alaska.

They spent five freezing months in and around Pt. Barrow, Alaska, looking for the bowling trophies in igloos but that didn't come to anything.

And it was very hard to find filling stations to hold up in that area, so the Logan brothers had to temporarily give up their occupation and were then reduced to stealing blubber to eat from unattended igloos.

Finally, they met an old Eskimo who told them that he had heard about some statues of silver and gold little men who were pitching little balls with their hands and seemed happy doing so.

"Those sound like bowling trophies," one of the Logan brothers said to another Logan brother, who was standing there freezing in a snowstorm. The third brother did not want a beer.

"Do you know what a bowling trophy is?" a Logan asked the old Eskimo.

"You mean, prize given for thunderball that runs on wood?"

"Yes! That's a bowling trophy!" the Logan exclaimed.

"Try San Francisco," the Eskimo said, pointing the way south through the falling snow.

Beautiful
American Night

The actress with the big breasts was very uncomfortable
all the time that she was being "interviewed" by Johnny
Carson because he kept making leering remarks but the
audience enjoyed them and so did John. Normally, he had
turned Johnny Carson off by this time of the night but he
had no intention of turning Johnny off as long as he was
making all these funny remarks about this girl's tits.

Johnny Carson was somehow, it seemed almost mirac-
ulous to John, able to work in a sentence about a cow in
another context. He didn't suggest in anyway that the girl
was a cow but when he said the word cow, everybody
looked at her tits and laughed heartily.

John tried not to wake up Patricia with his laughter.

Bob stumbled over a curb as they, he and Constance,

went to cross the street. He was thrown off balance but Constance caught his elbow, so he didn't fall.

"I almost fell," he said.

Constance thought he was going to say something else but he didn't, so they continued walking in silence back to their apartment.

The *Greek Anthology* Telephone Call

The telephone rang just as the Logan brother's hand touched the receiver and he picked it up without any hesitation in one motion as if the telephone had been ringing all the time.

"Yes," he said.

"..."

"I'm one of them," he said.

"..."

"The very same," he said.

"..."

"Thank you," he said.

"..."

"On Chestnut," he said.

"..."

"Yes," he said.

"..."

"I appreciate it," he said.

"..."

"Yes," he said.

"..."

"Thank you," he said.

"..."

"Any time," he said.

The Logan brother hung up.

Lost

Bob fumbled open the front door of the apartment building with his key and they went upstairs to their apartment on the top floor. The light was out on the stairs. It had burned out the day before and hadn't been replaced yet. Either Patricia or Constance would take care of it. Somehow they always ended up replacing the light in the hall.

Bob fumbled open the door to their apartment and they went in and took off their coats. The apartment was ablaze with lights.

"Who left the lights on?" Bob said.

Constance didn't answer him.

She went into the kitchen and got a glass of water. She was still thirsty from having been gagged so long earlier in the evening.

Bob wandered aimlessly around the apartment, not even knowing that he was doing it.

"Are you sleepy?" Constance asked Bob as he wandered past her on one of his directionless journeys.

"I guess so," he said.

"Then let's go to bed," Constance said.

"I'd like to read a little from the *Greek Anthology*," Bob said. "Before I go to sleep."

He started to look around the apartment for the book. He looked in the kitchen. He couldn't find it there. He looked in the bedroom but it wasn't there either, so it had to be in the front room. He went into the front room expecting to find the book there.

Constance brushed her teeth and then went into the bedroom and started getting undressed for bed. She was very tired. She was too young to be as tired as she felt.

"Constance?" Bob called to her from the front room.

"What is it, Bob?"

"Have you seen the *Greek Anthology*? It has to be in the front room but I can't find it."

The *Greek Anthology* was on a small table next to the bed. Constance was staring at it.

"No," she said.

"It has to be some place," Bob said. "It just couldn't have disappeared off the face of the earth."

Constance finished taking her clothes off. She could hear Bob looking for the *Greek Anthology* in the kitchen. She didn't care. She got into bed. She always slept without any clothes on.

He gave up in the kitchen and came into the bedroom.

156

Constance was lying in bed with the covers pulled close up around her neck.

"Hey, there it is," Bob said happily, spotting the *Greek Anthology* on the table beside the bed. "I knew it had to be some place."

Near the End
of the Trail

The Logan brothers packed their suitcase. That took about ten seconds and they checked out of the hotel. The one Logan brother had the .22 pistol in his pocket.

Their car which looked a lot older and battered than it did when they left home three years ago was parked across the street from the hotel.

One of the brothers put the suitcase in the trunk next to a full five-gallon can of gasoline. His brothers were already in the front seat of the car when he got in beside them.

"What's the address?" they asked him.

"It's on Chestnut Street."

"Did he tell you how to get there?"

They had already had this conversation before in the

hotel room after the one brother had hung up the telephone. They were just repeating it again because it made
them happy. Soon they would have their bowling
trophies back.

"Yeah, turn left here at Pine Street, then go down it
for a ways and I'll show you where to turn. We turn at
Fillmore."

They drove slowly down Pine Street toward the recov-
ery of their stolen bowling trophies. They didn't say anything to each other. Two of the brothers were lost in
thoughts of seeing their beloved bowling trophies again.
The other brother was thinking about murder.

Five Minutes
to One

"One more minute," John told himself. *"I'm going to watch Johnny Carson just one more minute."*

There were only a few moments left of the program which ended at 1 A.M. John always liked to turn Johnny Carson off before the program was over. Whenever he watched the entire program he always felt a little bad. He liked to be in control of his television watching and not a prisoner of it, so he always felt a little bad if he watched the entire Johnny Carson show. Normally, he just watched twenty or thirty minutes of it and that was enough to get him sleepy, to kind of wind his mind down from the day's activities.

He turned the set off just a few seconds before Johnny Carson said good night to millions of Americans and John didn't feel bad at all. He was the dictator of his television watching and had triumphed again.

He turned the light out and cuddled close to the warm sleeping form of Patricia.

"Good night," he said, though she couldn't hear him.

Millions of people heard Johnny Carson say good night.

Toward Meeting the Logan Brothers

The Logan brothers parked their car across the street from the apartment where Patricia and John and Constance and Bob lived. It was a three-story building with a laundry on the bottom floor. Then there was Patricia and John's apartment that occupied the entire second floor, and Constance and Bob's apartment was the third floor. There was a locked front door on the street level and then a long flight of stairs that led up to the apartments above.

The Logan brothers walked over to the building. They looked around. The street was very quiet because it was just a few moments after one in the morning. The street had had a lot of traffic earlier in the evening but the traffic had pretty much trailed away into only an occasional car after midnight.

"This is the building," a Logan said to nobody because his brothers already knew that this was the building. He tried the door. "It's locked," he said.

One of them reached into his pocket and took out a short piece of stiff plastic, something left over from the days when they did minor crime things before they found their niche: filling station holdups.

He slipped the piece of plastic into the door where the lock was and pushed the bolt back with the piece of plastic and opened the door in a quick motion.

The Logan brothers were inside.

They started carefully up the stairs. It was very dark. They didn't want to make any more noise than was necessary.

"*This is it,*" one of them whispered, halfway up the stairs toward the first apartment.

"*Shut up,*" another Logan whispered.

The Dice Thrown

Bob sat down on the bed and started reading the *Greek Anthology* to Constance.

"It's late," she said, trying gently to protest, but it didn't make any difference because Bob didn't hear her. He just kept on reading.

" 'A wattle basket full of the stalks of fine white celery,' " he read to her. Then he paused and said, "I wonder what a wattle basket is. What's a wattle basket, honey?"

"It's a basket woven out of twigs and sticks," Constance sighed. She slowly closed her eyes. She lay there on the bed with her eyes closed.

"Is this the apartment?" the Logan with the gun whispered as they all stood there on the landing beside the first apartment. The landing was dark, so they couldn't see any number on the door.

"What's the number?"

The comic-book-reading Logan who'd answered the telephone was thinking very hard as his brother struck a match to expose a copper number 2 on the front door to the flickering flame of the match.

"It's number 1," he suddenly remembered.

"But this number says 2," was the whispering from his brother.

"It's number 1. I tell you. 1. It's 1," whispering.

"Then the apartment upstairs must be number 1," whispering.

"Yeah, it has to be. If this is number 2, then number 1 must be upstairs," whispering.

"What's number 2 doing down here? Shouldn't number 1 be down here and number 2 up there?" whispering.

"All I know is that it's number 1. That's where the bowling trophies are. Let's go up there and get them," whispering.

"OK, but it seems funny to me," whispering.

One of the Logan brothers was not whispering. All he wanted was a can of beer.

On a slightly drunken evening a few months ago, Patricia and John decided to play a little joke on Constance and Bob by switching the numbers on the apartments while they were out.

They thought that it would be very funny for the first apartment in the building to be number 2 and the second apartment to be number 1.

Constance did not think it was funny when she saw it. Bob was puzzled. "I thought we lived in apartment 2," he said, staring at the number 1 on the door to their apartment.

"It's all right," Constance said.

"But it seems strange to me," Bob said.

"Don't think about it," Constance said, not liking it but somehow they never got around to changing the numbers back. One thing or another kept them away from it.

The Logan brothers moved stealthily up the next flight of stairs to Constance and Bob's apartment.

"See, here's number 1," the comic-book-reading Logan whispered triumphantly.

"Number 1," his brother whispered, taking the pistol out of his pocket. He wasn't saying it to anybody. He was just saying it to himself. It had been three years long enough to be lifetimes and perhaps they were. "Number 1," again whispered.

There was a moment of silence as the brothers stood in front of the door. They didn't move. They didn't say anything. They just stood there.

"Listen to this, Constance," Bob said. "This may have something to do with us." Bob had gotten Constance's attention by saying that.

" 'The dice of Love are madnesses and melees,' " Bob quoted from the *Greek Anthology* as the Logan brothers kicked in the front door and ran into the apartment looking for the bowling trophies and the first one in ran down the hall into the bedroom shouting, "BOWLING TROPHY THIEVES DIE!" and shot the two people, one of whom was sitting on the bed reading from a book while the other one was lying in bed, listening to him as he read with her eyes closed.

"Searching for an Octopus" or Epilogue

Q: What about the Logan sisters?
A: Forget them.